The Daddy Book

TODD PARR

LB
Megan Tingley Books
LITTLE, BROWN AND COMPANY
New York Boston

Little, Brown and Company

Hachette Book Group
237 Park Avenue, New York, NY 10017
Visit our website at www.lb-kids.com

Little, Brown and Company is a division of Hachette Book Group, Inc.
The Little, Brown name and logo are trademarks of Hachette Book Group, Inc.

First Paperback Edition: June 2010
Originally published in hardcover in April 2002 by Little, Brown and Company

Library of Congress Cataloging-in-Publication Data

Parr, Todd.
The daddy book / by Todd Parr. — 1st ed.
p.cm.
"Megan Tingley Books."
Summary: Represents a variety of fathers, with lots of hair and little hair, making cookies and buying doughnuts, camping out and taking naps, and hugging and kissing their children.
ISBN 978-0-316-07039-3 (pb) / ISBN 978-0-316-60799-5 (hc)
[1. Fathers— Fiction.] I. Title
PZ7.P2447 Fdg 2002
[E] — dc21 2001029097

10 9 8 7 6 5 4 3 2

QUAL

Manufactured in China

This book is dedicated to
all the different kinds of dads
who have worked so hard to make
life a little bit easier with their
unconditional love and support.

Especially MY DAD!

Love,
Todd

Some daddies take
pictures of you

Some daddies draw pictures of you

Some daddies wear suits

Some daddies wear two different socks

Some daddies sing in the shower

Some daddies sing to you in bed

All daddies like to try

new things with you!

Some daddies work at home

Some daddies work far away

Some daddies like to build sand castles

Some daddies like to cover you with sand

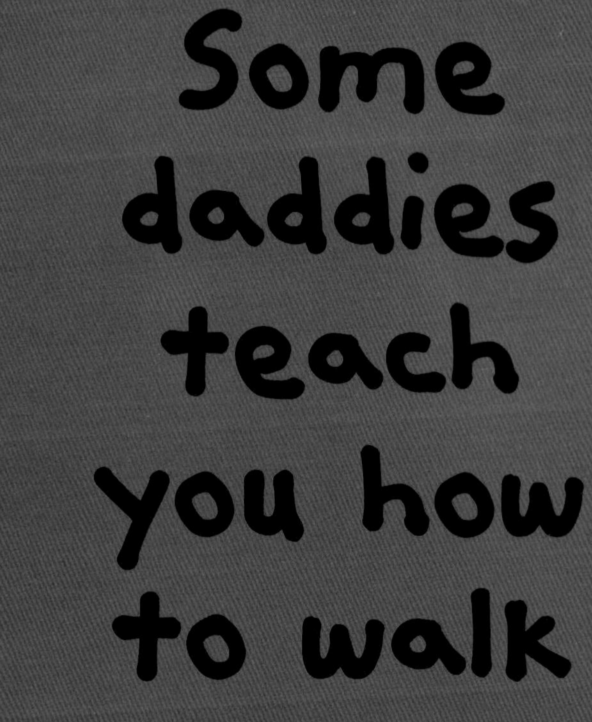

Some daddies teach you how to walk

Some daddies teach you
how to ride a
skateboard

All daddies like to watch you sleep!

Some daddies have a lot of hair

Some daddies have
a little hair

Some daddies
play in your
tr hous

Some daddies have
tea parties
with you

Some daddies
make cookies

Some daddies stop for doughnuts

All daddies love to kiss

and hug you!

Some daddies walk
you to school

Some daddies walk you to the bus

Some daddies like to camp out with you and the dog

Some daddies like to take naps with you

All daddies want you
to be who you are!